D1186666

"Come closer, my child," said the old man to his grandchild, "and I will tell you the story of a kiss. There are many sorts of kisses — some are like feathers, others are snowflakes and others leaves…"

TO KISSES OF ALL COLOURS AND COUNTRIES
FROM WHOMEVER THEY'RE SENT
TO WHOMEVER THEY'RE GIVEN
M.B. and T.V.

MARCIAL BÓO

The Butterfly Kiss

Illustrated by Tim Vyner

VICTOR GOLLANCZ · LONDON

Once there was a beautiful butterfly kiss which fluttered among the trees of the forest. But the butterfly kiss was not really happy. "My family and friends have found homes," it said, "and now I'm all alone. I wonder if anyone wants me?"

The kiss floated off through the trees to try to find a home. It drifted past a sleepy-looking tiger, lying on a rock in the shade of a tall tree. "Would you like a kiss?" it asked the tiger.

"Not just now," said the tiger. "I'm settling down for my morning nap. I'm far too tired and sleepy to kiss anyone."

"Oh dear," said the kiss. "I'll have to find my home somewhere else."

"Good luck," yawned the tiger.

The kiss darted away from the trees. Down it
flew to a fat elephant, who was splashing around
on the bank of a river.
"Would you like a kiss?" it asked the elephant.

"No thank you," said the elephant. "I've lots and lots of kisses stored up in my trunk and I don't need any more at the moment."

"Oh dear," said the kiss. "I'll have to find my home somewhere else."

"Goodbye," trumpeted the elephant.

The kiss blew away from the riverside and
swept up to the top of a high tree, where
a stork had built a nest.
"Would you like a kiss?" it asked the stork.

"Not yet," said the stork. "I'm sitting on my eggs,
but they won't hatch for another few days.
I shan't need any kisses until then."
"Oh dear," said the kiss. "I'll have to find my
home somewhere else."
"See you soon," whistled the stork.

Away wafted the kiss. It soared across the river
to a crocodile, who was basking on some mudflats.
"Would you like a kiss?" it asked the crocodile.

"Not likely," said the crocodile. "I don't like kisses.
I just snap, snap, snap with my mighty jaws.
I don't like kisses at all."
"Oh dear," said the kiss. "I'll have to find my
home somewhere else."
"And don't come back," gnashed the crocodile.

The kiss swerved quickly away from the
crocodile and skimmed into the long grass
nearby, where a hare was hiding.
"Would you like a kiss?" it asked the hare.

"I'm afraid not," said the hare. "We don't kiss.
When we like someone very much, we wiggle
our noses up and down and rub them together."
"Oh dear," said the kiss. "I'll have to find my
home somewhere else."
"Farewell," twitched the hare.

The kiss glided away over the fields. It flitted
up to the branches of a tree, where a bat was
hanging. "Would you like a kiss?" it asked the bat.
"I don't think so," said the bat. "The sun is
going down and I've just woken up. I won't need
any kisses until my bedtime in the morning."
"Oh dear," said the kiss. "I'll have to find my
home somewhere else."
"Good evening to you," twittered the bat.

The kiss wondered if anyone wanted a kiss.
The tiger, the elephant and the stork didn't.
The crocodile, the hare and the bat didn't.
"Where can I go now?" it cried.
"Try over there," said a white cow with large horns,
who was ambling slowly into the village.
Not far away, the kiss saw a
light in a window.

The kiss floated through the window. Inside
the room was an old man, who was telling
a story to a child.
"Would you like a kiss?" the kiss asked the child.
"Yes please," said the child. "Yes! Yes! Yes!"
So the kiss fluttered happily between the old
man and his grandchild, as they gave each
other a goodnight kiss.

First published in Great Britain 1995
by Victor Gollancz
An imprint of the Cassell Group
Wellington House, 125 Strand, London WC2R 0BB

Text copyright © Marcial Bóo 1995
Illustrations copyright © Tim Vyner 1995

The right of Marcial Bóo and Tim Vyner to be identified as
authors of this work has been asserted by them in accordance with
the Copyright, Designs and Patents Act, 1988.

A catalogue record for this book is
available from the British Library.

ISBN 0 575 05977 X

*All rights reserved. No reproduction, copy or transmission of
this publication in any form or by any means, electronic or
mechanical including photocopying, recording or any information
storage or retrieval system, may be made without prior written
permission from the publishers and this publication, or any part of
it, shall not, by way of trade or otherwise, be made up for sale,
or re-sold or otherwise circulated in any other form than
that in which it is published.*

Printed in Hong Kong